the upside-down fish

For Mum, for our upside-down fish. —K. L.

For Kester, my everything. —L. M.

the UPSide-down fish

ME AND MY BEST FREND

Written by
Kate Louise

Illustrated by
Laura Matine

Sky Pony Press
New York

Upside-down Fish swims upside-down.

Down is up . . .

. . . and up is down.

He lives at the pet store in a tank full of fish that swim the right-way up.

Upside-down Fish is very lonely. He doesn't like being one of a kind.

None of the other fish let him join in with their right-way up fishy swimming.

When children come to choose
a fish for a pet, they never pick
Upside-down Fish to take home.

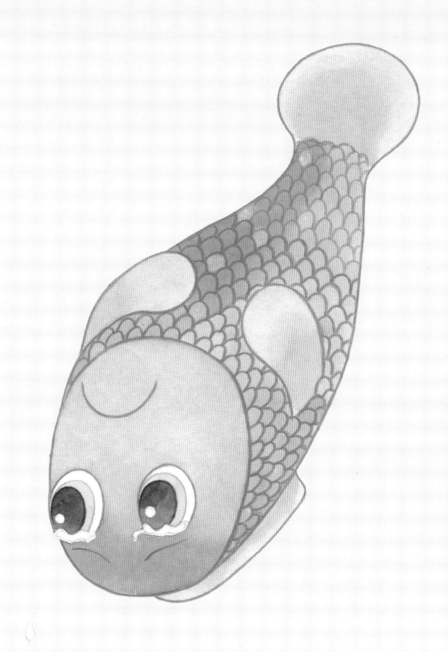

He doesn't think they
even notice him.

One very dull day, Upside-down Fish
spent his morning swimming around
and around the tank. Then he blew
bubbles in the afternoon.

Later, the tank was opened and food
fell from above (or from below, in
Upside-down Fish's case).

The fish dashed up (or is it down?) and gobbled up the food. The water rocked from side to side. Upside-down Fish was left confused and floating in a large empty space. And at that exact moment, a child came into the store to choose a fish.

"I want that one," the girl said.
"The one that's swimming
upside-down!"

splash!

A net plopped into the
water and Upside-down
Fish was finally scooped up!
He was put into a bag and
taken out of the pet store.

The world looked very strange to Upside-down Fish. You see, the ground was up above and the sky was down below.

Upside-down Fish
had a brand new tank
to call home.

But, oh no! All the fish in the tank were swimming the right-way up.

Upside-down Fish worried that the fish wouldn't accept him, just like the ones back at the pet store.

But when Upside-down Fish
was placed into the tank, he
got a very warm welcome!

The right-way up fish wanted to know what the world looked like upside-down. Some of them even flapped their fins and flipped onto their backs to see for themselves.

Upside-down Fish was finally happy and realized that it's okay not to be the same as all the other fish. In fact, it's quite nice to be a little bit different!

After all, in a tank full of right-way up fish and only one upside-down fish, who do you think stands out more?

Sky Pony Press books may be purchased in bulk at special discounts for sales promotion, corporate gifts, fund-raising, or educational purposes. Special editions can also be created to specifications. For details, contact the Special Sales Department, Sky Pony Press, 307 West 36th Street, 11th Floor, New York, NY 10018 or info@skyhorsepublishing.com.

Sky Pony® is a registered trademark of Skyhorse Publishing, Inc.®, a Delaware corporation.

Visit our website at www.skyponypress.com.

10 9 8 7 6 5 4 3 2 1

Manufactured in China, October 2014
This product conforms to CPSIA 2008

Library of Congress Cataloging-in-Publication Data

Louise, Kate.
The upside-down fish / written by Kate Louise; illustrated by Laura Matine.
pages cm
Summary: Ignored by the other fish in the pet store, Upside-down Fish feels lonely until a child takes him home, he meets new fish who are friendly, and he discovers that being different makes him special.
ISBN 978-1-62914-628-7 (hardback)
[1. Fishes—Fiction. 2. Individuality—Fiction. 3. Self-acceptance—Fiction.] I. Matine, Laura, illustrator. II. Title.
PZ7.L93143Up 2015
[E—dc23
2014023912

Cover design by Danielle Ceccolini
Cover illustration credit Laura Matine

Ebook ISBN: 978-1-63220-230-7